GOOD NIGHT

by Elizabeth Coatsworth
pictures by Jose Aruego

The Macmillan Company, New York, New York

The Macmillan Company, 866 Third Avenue, New York, N.Y. 10022
Collier-Macmillan Canada Ltd., Toronto, Ontario
Library of Congress catalog card number: 79-175596
Printed in the United States of America   1 2 3 4 5 6 7 8 9 10

The four-color illustrations were prepared as pen-and-ink line drawings with halftone overlays for gray, tan, blue and brown. The typeface is Linofilm Optima.

With
dearest
love
for
I. R. C.

The sun is setting.
How slowly it sets.

The darkness is coming.
How softly it comes.

Look!
There is a star!

Can a star see?

Yes, it sees the mother bird
on her nest.
Her wings spread wide
to cover blue eggs.

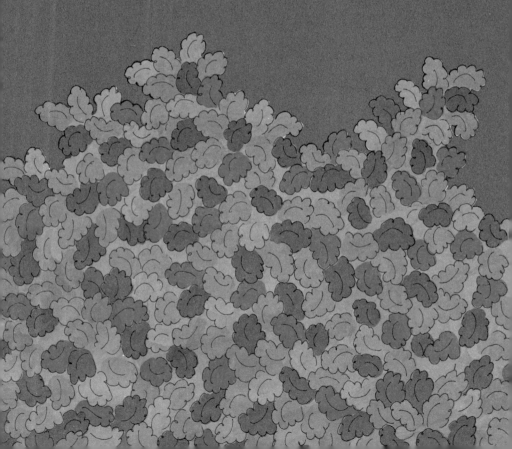

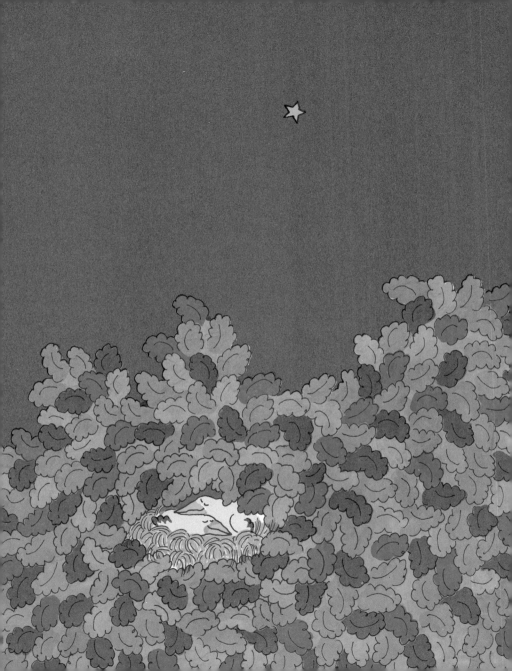

It sees the mare
standing close to her colt.

It sees the dog
in a circle of puppies.

It sees the cat family
under the stove.

But can a star see
under the stove?

Yes, yes! A star can see
even under a stove.

It sees the child
going to bed.

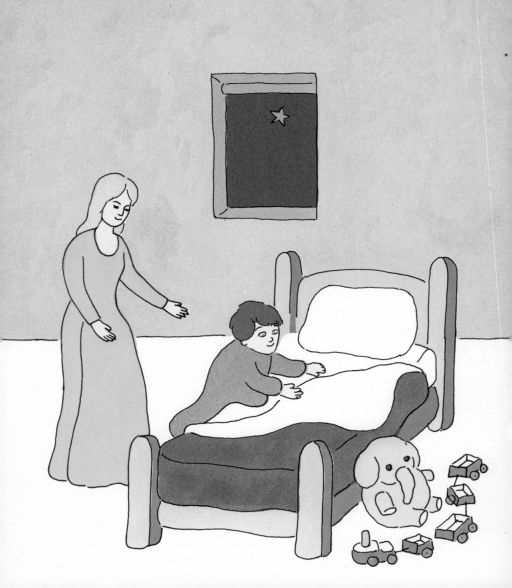

He moves slowly, slowly,
like the sun.

He moves very softly,
like the darkness coming.

The star has seen this
often and often.

U.S. 1688216

The child is sleepy.
Yawning, he says,

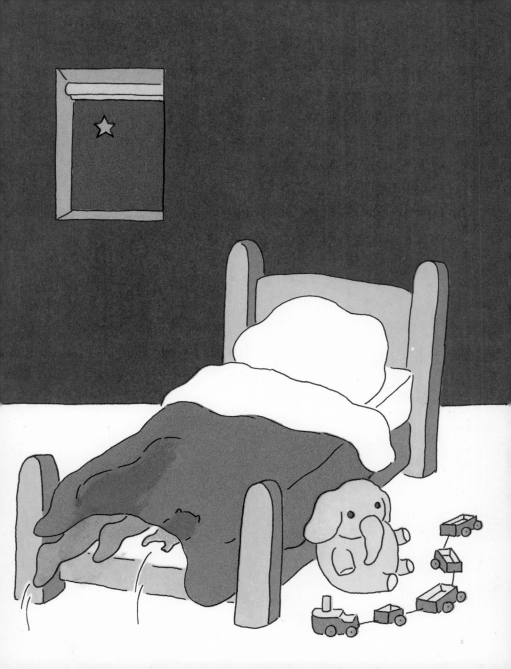

"Good night."